Book Belongs To:

This book is dedicated to all of those facing demons or feeling dammed, both inside and out, in the hope that the good will always triumph in the end.

Never give up hope of finding help, or a cure, as it can always be found if you only take time to look.

In the middle of the roaring Ocean
A large ship with dark sails caould be seen
Nobody knew where it was heading
But we could see exactly where it had been

This ship appeared broken and decaying
And almost everyone had heard the tale
Of the most frightening Pirate ever imagined
Who enjoyed leaving shipwrecks in his trail

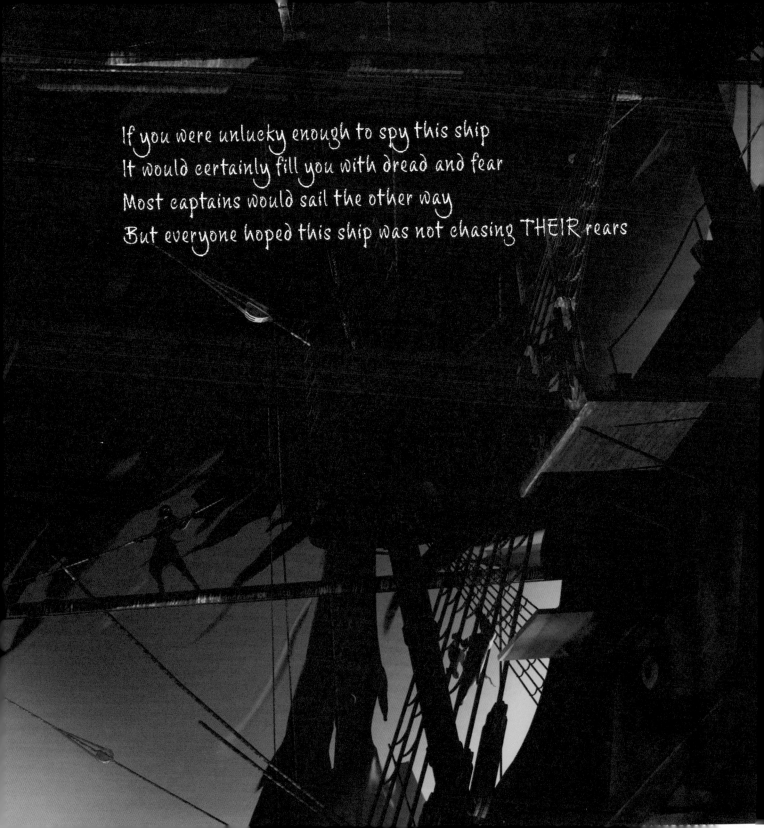

If you were unlucky enough to spy this ship
It would certainly fill you with dread and fear
Most captains would sail the other way
But everyone hoped this ship was not chasing THEIR rears

THE FLYING
DUTCHMAN

This ship was named "The Flying Dutchman"
And it was manned by a terrible crew
Made up of the dead and the dammed
And their captain, everybody knew

"Vladimir" was the captain's name
A character who struck fear across all 7 seas
He was no normal Pirate or Man
As would bring almost any Captain to his knees

"Vlad" as he liked to be called
Was very tall and surprisingly quick
On his face was always a crooked smile
And on his hands, Claws extra-long and thick

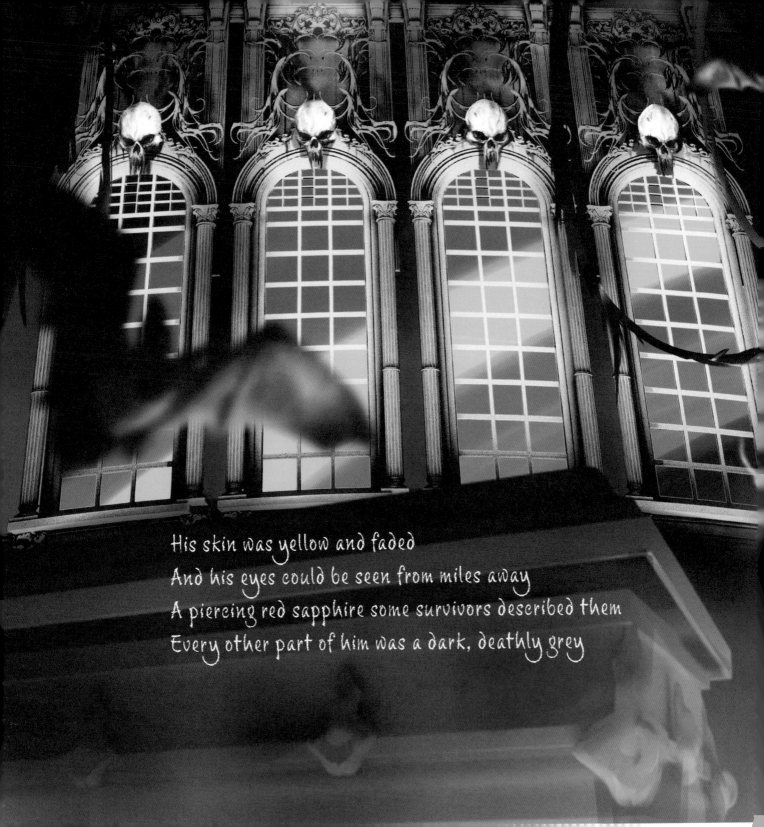

His skin was yellow and faded
And his eyes could be seen from miles away
A piercing red sapphire some survivors described them
Every other part of him was a dark, deathly grey

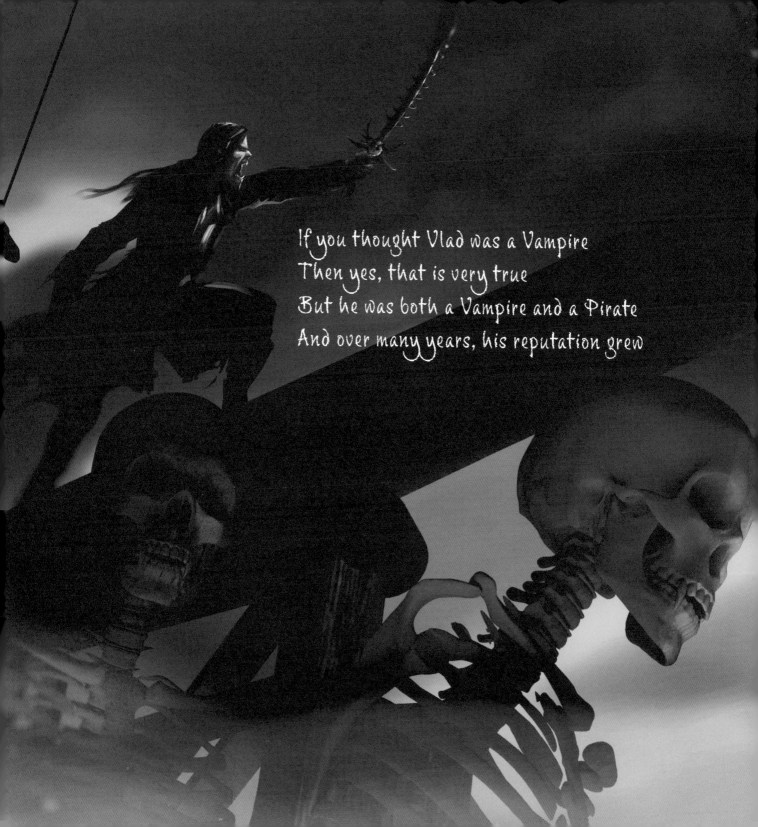

If you thought Vlad was a Vampire
Then yes, that is very true
But he was both a Vampire and a Pirate
And over many years, his reputation grew

Vlad was a terrifying Vampire
But he could never set foot in the sun
A secret, very well hidden
Yet a better pirate, there was none

This meant Vlad was best in darkness
And planned all of his attacks at night
This gave him the greatest advantage
And best chance to win every fight

Vlad did not ever believe
That one day, he may finally lose
So, we introduce our muscular hero
The fearless Captain Hughes

Captain Aiden Hughes was from Ireland
But across the world, he had fame
He was the most successful Pirate hunter
And catching baddies was his favourite game

Captain Hughes had searched for years
To hunt down Vlad and his crew
He could feel himself getting closer
And each day, his anticipation grew

The "RMS Fortuna" ship
Was owned by Captain Hughes
And he was standing at the helm
When his crew bellowed some glorious news

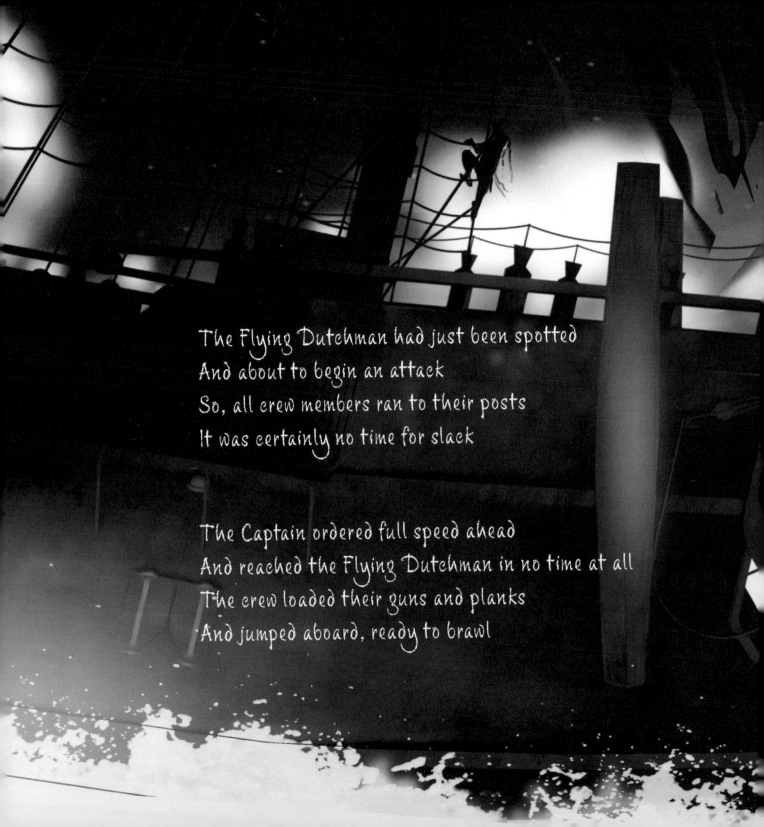

The Flying Dutchman had just been spotted
And about to begin an attack
So, all crew members ran to their posts
It was certainly no time for slack

The Captain ordered full speed ahead
And reached the Flying Dutchman in no time at all
The crew loaded their guns and planks
And jumped aboard, ready to brawl

Captain Hughes was the first to land
And swiftly drew out his sword
He cut down 3 enemies in 1 swing
And watched them fall to the floor

This was when the Captain realised
That this terrifying crew lived up to their name
All 3 cursed crew returned to their feet
And made an attack for him once again

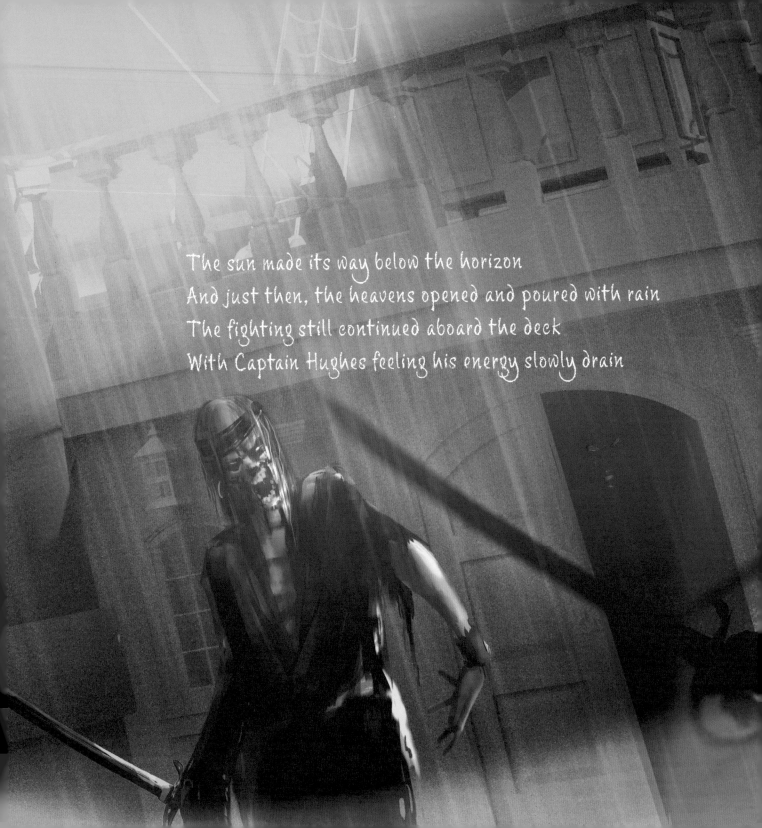

The sun made its way below the horizon
And just then, the heavens opened and poured with rain
The fighting still continued aboard the deck
With Captain Hughes feeling his energy slowly drain

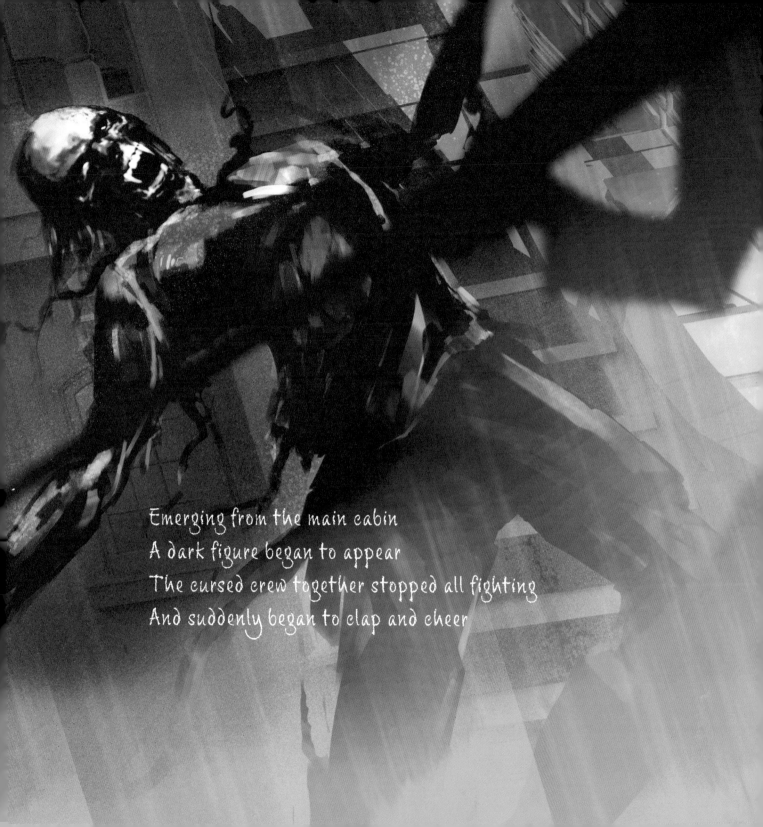

Emerging from the main cabin
A dark figure began to appear
The cursed crew together stopped all fighting
And suddenly began to clap and cheer

Vlad walked towards Captain Hughes
And drew out a sword made from bone
The Captain stood tall and did not flinch
And walked forward, meeting Vlad alone

"Your time is over Pirate" shouted the Captain
"So now prepare to finally lose"
"But you haven't fought someone like me" Vlad replied
Letting out a crooked smile and looking amused

They both ran towards each other
And soon, a massive clash of bone and steel
Captain Hughes drew first blood
But Vlad immediately began to heal

The battle between these warriors raged on
Captain Hughes matched each slash and swing
Until a single fateful moment
When he heard a loud "crack" and sharp "ping"

Aiden looked down to find his sword in pieces
With another deadly blow from Vlad on its way
But thankfully, Captain Hughes acted swiftly
And out came his silver dagger to save the day

His dagger deflected the incoming swing
But the force of it took him to his knees
He then spotted a gap in Vlad's defence
And performed a forward roll with such ease

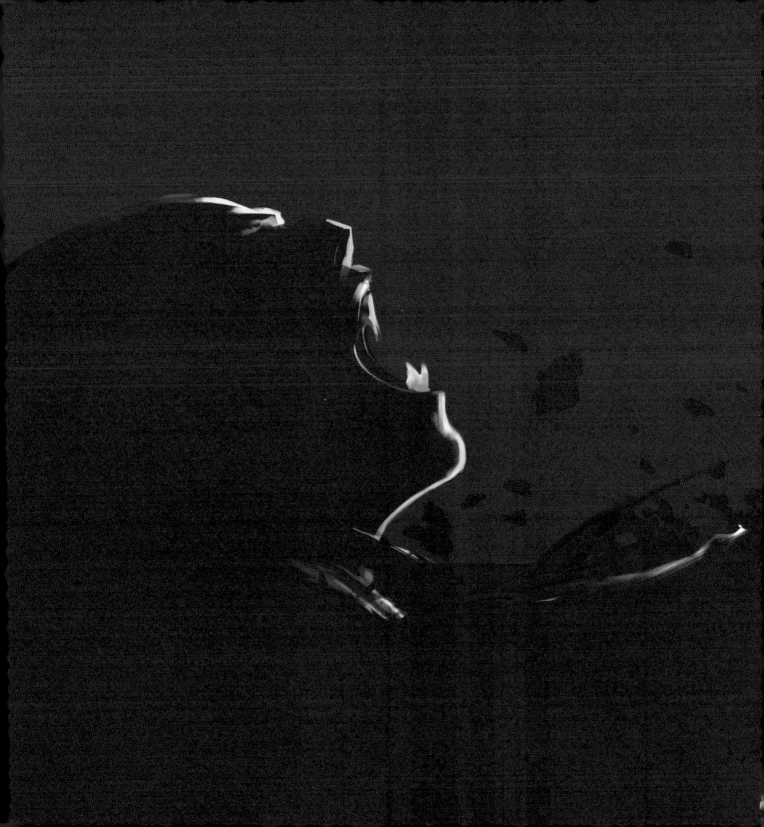

This caught our villain by surprise
As Vlad looked down to see a dagger in his chest
There was a look of shock and wonder on his face
As he realised this time, he had been second best

At that moment, Vlad looked at Captain Hughes
And vanished into a cloud of dust
Captain Hughes looked down at this dagger
In which his father told him to always place his trust

Vlad's former crew swore new loyalty
And Captain Hughes made them a promise that day
That he would find a cure for their curse
And help them to find peace in some way

This Captain lived up to that promise
He found a cure and helped fix this crew
The seas remained peaceful for many years
But what happened to Vlad, nobody knew...

Published by Lazy Leprechaun Publishing

Lazy Leprechaun Publishing

Illustrated by Eduardo Paj

Self-published on Amazon by Conor Cassidy 2021

About the Author

After 4 previously successful books, I found myself still writing and coming up with some new ideas as and when I get some time (something not so easy to come by these days).
I loved the mix of the pirates and vampires stories from games and videos and thought, why not try and combine some storylines? It will be something new and unique that I hope everyone will love. Slightly darker than my previous books, and using a new illustrator for this one will be a test of skill and creativity but I hope it is still as enjoyable as the others.

I welcome all feedback and suggestions for improvement and of course, suggested future endeavours.

For more information and to stay up to date, please follow me below:

Twitter: https://twitter.com/CCassCreations

Facebook: https://www.facebook.com/conorcassidycreations/

Website: http://www.conorcassidycreations.co.uk/

Lazy Leprechaun Publishing

CONOR CASSIDY CREATIONS

Other Books by the Author

Printed in Great Britain
by Amazon